100-Word Stories for Reflection

WINSTON WATERTON

100-Word Stories for Reflection

THEA
social promotion association

This book is dedicated to:
My great ancestors
The light-hearted people in the world
The creative souls
Rosella Robertazzi
Debra and Sharon Waterton
My children, grandchildren and children not yet born
Stefano and Sonia Pizzaroni
Bob and Greta Gair
Leo Zampa
&
Elena Taborri
for encouraging and challenging me
to write 100-word stories,
helping to wake a dormant creative skill
residing in me.

Disclaimer

The stories are purely fictional and born from unexpected flashes of images and words from my imagination and intuition.

I would like to write about real events in my life, but I do not want anyone to sue me. I will take those stories to my grave. As my dear mother used to say in a soft and sweet voice, "Winston, there are some things that must be left unsaid and taken to the ancestral world." I agree with her.

Contents

Introduction

It is a pleasure to share 21 of my creative stories for reflection. The stories are one hundred words or less. Most stories are funny and terrible at the same time, but wisdom can be found in them with considered thought.

You need to have a sense of humour to read my stories. Read them individually and in groups and have a discussion about what you have learnt.

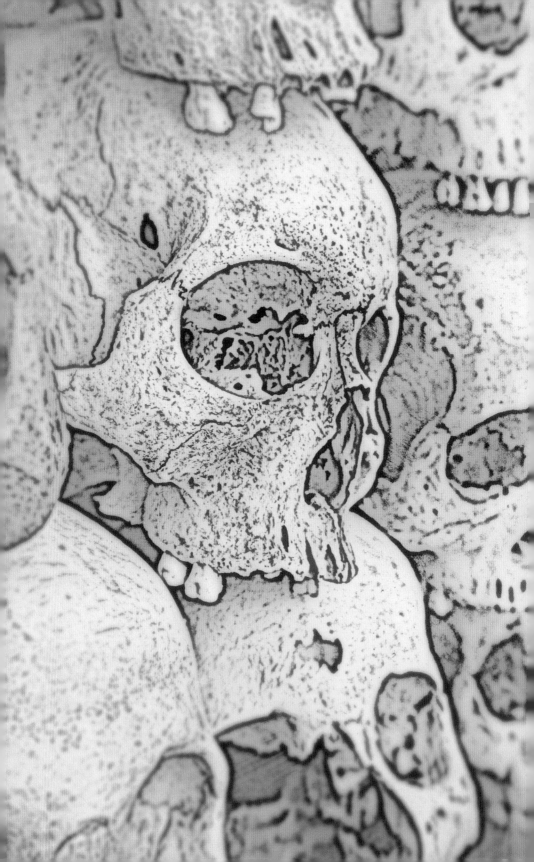

Great Pride Before Fearless Beauty

Last week Napoleon, the most feared army general in Europe killed 1,000 people. Yesterday 5,000 dead. Today he faced his first female opponent, the beautiful, majestic and fearless African Queen Candance.

She sent her ferocious warriors to the frontline to give Napoleon a two-metre bow and arrow gift with a message, "Someone has to stop your conquest. Cross my frontline if you think you can win!"

Rather than risk losing a battle to a woman, Napoleon decided to return to Europe claiming he had conquered enough of Africa and wanted to spend more time with his family.

A Stone Heart Found Peace

Natalie was cold-hearted and bitter. Her face looked like 10 kilometres of bad road. If looks could kill many people would die when their eyes crossed hers.

Natalie was very angry with her ex-lover who left her for a younger and more beautiful woman. Every time she thought about her sad love life, she would destroy many things in her home until there was nothing else to break.

Yet, there was one thing that brought her peace; her calm, furry cat. His purring always made her feel as light as a feather, as if it understood her feelings.

The Power of an Intuitive Kiss

Natalie and Napoleon were on a 10-day religious retreat in the luscious hills of Bologna, Italy, seeking spiritual upliftment.

They had fallen in love with each other at first sight, but they were both nervous and scared to tell each other. They both remembered being blinded by love before; romantic relationships made in heaven that later turned into hell.

However, on the fourth day of the retreat, Napoleon was walking past Natalie and the voice of God in his head quietly told him to kiss her. Natalie was mesmerised, fell, hit her head on the ground and died.

The Decluttering Day

Napoleon had thousands of excuses
not to clear the mountain of clutter in his
home. Yet, doing this and other healthy
lifestyle changes could have helped resolve
his depression, and given him a fresh start
in life, the counsellor said. However,
he refused.

Napoleon lived in an earthquake region of
Europe and one day, the earthquake was
stronger than previous months. Terrified
people had already left their homes,
but not Napoleon, he was adamant about
remaining and was buried alive
from the tremors.

The priest said that "nature has a way of
helping people to move on from their lives."

Natalie woke up one morning and decided not to be afraid anymore. Not to fear criticism from others, especially from loved ones, which was crushing her self-esteem.

She walked into the bathroom with a new level of consciousness and liked who she saw in the mirror. She realised that the

After the Stormy Clouds

biggest psychological and emotional weights she was carrying were self-criticism, self-doubt, self-pity and an enormous lack of self-love.

She looked out of the window at the stormy clouds said happily, "I am ready to face the hurricanes of life with my head raised high."

the Sunshine Appears

Passionate Love

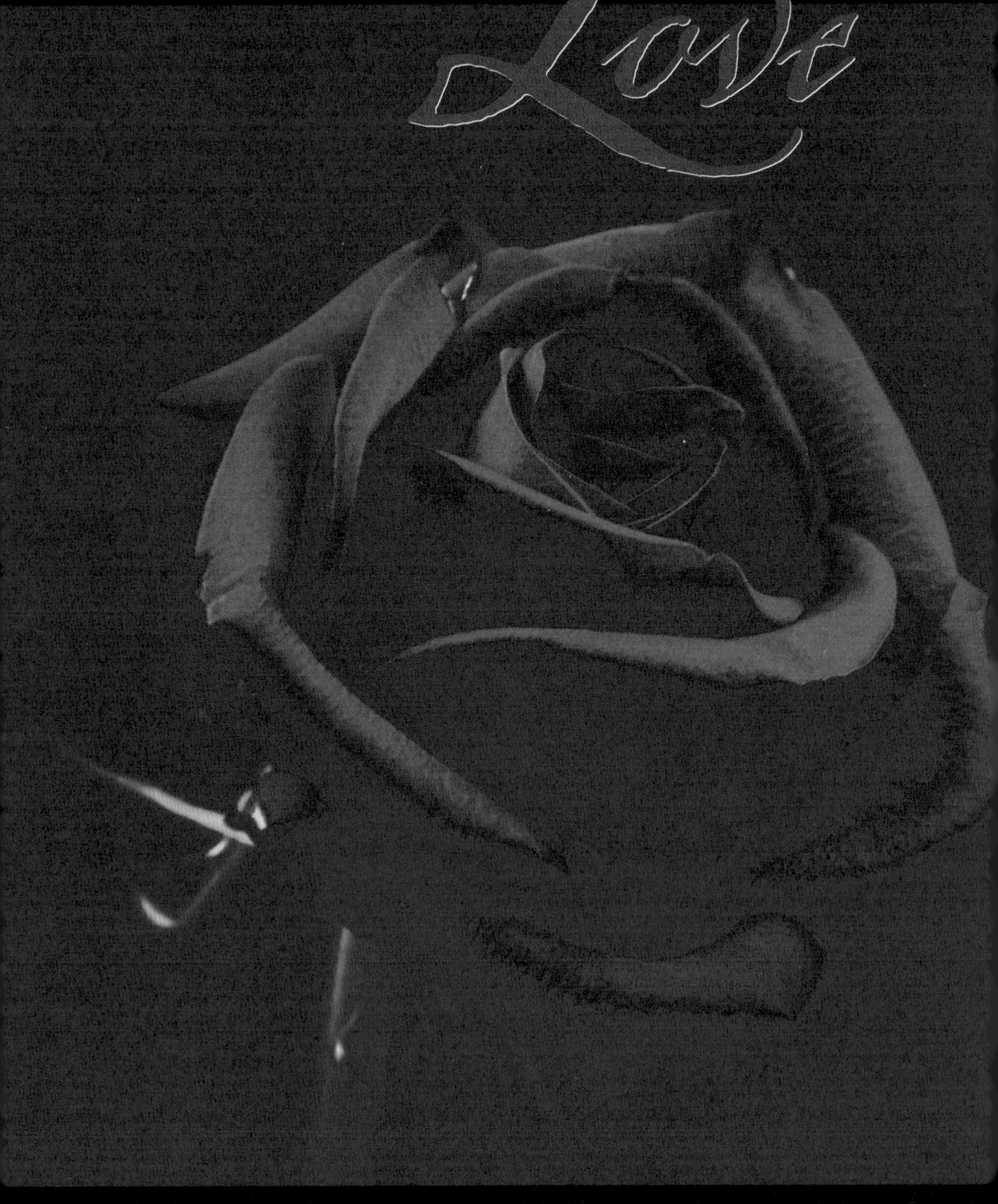

*N*apoleon was a devoted husband and family man. Natalie, his wife, said to all who would hear that he was a loyal man, her one and only love that made her heart melt. In her eyes, her beautiful, charming, generous husband could do no wrong.

After five years of marriage, she caught him naked making passionate love to the babysitter in their bed. She calmly watched their provocative sexual transactions and said to herself, "I have been blinded by love."

She took a slow walk to the kitchen, lit a cigarette, made a cup of tea, then loaded a shotgun.

Selfless Love

Natalie was a dedicated and devoted nurse with 30 years of experience. She spent her life caring for other people, sharing her warmth, love and kindness selflessly. She lived alone, had no time to socialise and no interest in finding a soulmate.

Natalie found nursing
to be very stressful, with
long hours and burdened
with bureaucracy; but she
loved making her patients
happy and meeting their
physical and spiritual needs.
However, after a brief illness, she
learnt that she was dying of cancer.
Sitting depressed in deep thought she said
to herself, "who is going to care for me?"

The Fastest Hands in the West

Natalie had the fastest hands in the Western World. She could make any food in the kitchen quickly with her skilled culinary skills. She was very efficient with the use of a knife and cut vegetables and meat quickly and fluidly.

Natalie was
Queen Elizabeth's
favourite chef and awarded
Master Chef of the Year three times.
Unfortunately, Natalie's strength was also her weakness. One day, she had an argument with Napoleon, her partner and lost her calm disposition.

Without thinking, she raised her hands and knocked Napoleon's head so hard he died before his body hit the floor.

CONSPIRACY
Hidden In Plain Sight

Natalie was the most intelligent sheep of the flock and able to see life's realities. She was a meticulous researcher and had a great eye for detail when studying humans.

One day while in the field, Natalie said to her flock, "I swear that dog and the man whistling nearby are working together." The other sheep laughed, saying that she was always talking about conspiracies.

The following week, the flock was guided to an abattoir and realised they were going to die. The flock cried "Bah! Natalie, you were right, the man and dog are collaborators in our demise."

Love that Heals and Kills

Napoleon had fallen
in love with Natalie.
She was dying from lung
cancer, but to the doctor's
surprise, the illness had
disappeared after a month
of intensive therapy.
Natalie thought it
was due to divine
intervention.
Elated Napoleon said it
was the power of love that
had extended her life.

A year later, Natalie had left Napoleon for another man. Shortly after, Napoleon was diagnosed with cancer and died.

At the funeral, the priest said that Napoleon died from a broken heart and warned others of the two sides of love; the love that heals and the love that kills.

The Killing

The door creaked as he slowly opened the bathroom door. Today will be my thirteenth victim Napoleon thought happily. "Roawh!" Napoleon shouted as he pounced on Natalie while she washed her hair. "Roawh!" Natalie shouted back as

EE FOUR FIVE

GHT NINE TEN

VE THIRTEEN FOU

NTEEN EIGHTEEN

TWENTY-TWO TW

Spree

she stabbed him in the stomach with her twelve-inch knife, looking at him fearlessly in the eye.

"This is not supposed to happen... the prey killing the hunter!" Napoleon said to Natalie as he experienced the shock of being caught off guard. Natalie smiled and said; "Today... 13 is the number of transformation," twisting the knife in his body.

THE KILLINGS IN TWO WORLDS

Natalie was the most wanted criminal in England and was finally caught red-handed killing a man in cold blood.

She picked up men from nightclubs, mesmerizing them with her seductive hypnotic skills, spiking their drinks, before slitting their throats in her luxurious penthouse apartment.

Natalie's last victim was a policeman. She was a suspect under investigation but the police arrived too late.

Today was her final day in her prison cell. "Any last words?" her executioner asked. Laughing hysterically as she was strapped to the electric chair, Natalie said grimly, "I will continue my killing in the ancestral world."

Death Comes With No Warning

Napoleon was a ruthless and manipulative man. He caused destruction everywhere he visited, destroying individuals and families. Many people tried to kill him unsuccessfully. Napoleon was a self-assured and confident man and believed nobody could kill him because of his impenetrable security.

Yesterday was Napoleon's funeral service. All his victims' family came to see his body laid to rest and asked how a well-protected murderer died.

Someone said that Mother Nature was fed up with Napoleon's evil behaviour, created a fierce thunderstorm and had struck him with 13 bolts of lightning. Nobody thought he would die this way.

The Oppressive Room

Natalie was a victim of domestic violence. She was locked up in a small room with a tiny barred window. Her husband abused her atrociously. One night he forced her to cook him some food. At that moment, Natalie realised that the abuse had to stop and she looked at the kitchen knife.

Natalie pleaded not guilty for reason of temporary insanity. Today she was released from prison after serving two years. In her autobiography, Natalie said that she was traumatised as a result of a serious crime, and she was a victim turned hero, liberating herself from oppressive hands.

Natalie was in prison for a crime that she didn't commit. She was framed by her unfaithful husband, who had killed his lover and told the police that Natalie had done it. Natalie told the judge that she would get her revenge in heaven or hell for the injustice she'd experienced.

After spending five years secretly digging a tunnel from her cell Natalie escaped and within days had found her husband and killed him. With a great sense of satisfaction, Natalie returned to the prison gate and asked for permission to enter and be returned to her same prison cell.

ONE DAY

OF CRAZY
FREEDOM

Natalie's choices in men were dreadful. She was told many times by close friends and mental health professionals, that she was living a false reality and that healthier ways of thinking were required.

One day, she was found lying on the floor looking like a million dollars, dressed in a sexy evening dress, and blood dripping from her eyes, nose and ears.

The coroner verdict was suicide. The psychiatrist said that he had lost a paying client. The mystic said that she had died twice from a broken heart, once in her dream world and again in her physical world.

Love Comes on Horseback
and Leaves on Foot

You Avoid Trouble
Yet Trouble Finds You

In ancient China, 630AD, peaceful times were brief. Frequent battles between warlords were common. 'Kill or be killed' was a popular saying. One day warriors visited a small quiet village and started destroying the market. Natalie, a calm and friendly dressmaker, begged them to stop their destruction to no avail.

The unrelentless warriors began destroying Natalie's shop. Natalie's sense of calmness quickly turned to rage, and with her two-strike fighting skills had killed all the warriors. The following day Natalie had disappeared. She knew that the news would quickly spread that she was the best fighter in the land.

Natalie was born into slavery. Brutality was her daily experience. Witnessing the murder of others was common, yet she listened to natural urges to be free and escaped from oppressive hands. She made a liberating decision to die fearlessly freeing other slaves and killing, unmercifully, those who stood in her way.

WANTED

Natalie didn't believe in oppressive laws,
only her law - The Law of Freedom.
The enslaving community called Natalie
a criminal. Natalie called
them pathetic, hypocrites
and psychopaths, and
proclaimed to the world,
"I am a natural-born rebel
with a beautiful purpose
called freedom.
Be free or die trying."

DEAD OR ALIVE

Death Does Not Knock

During the night Napoleon left his sleeping wife and went to the toilet. As he returned through the darkness, he saw a shadowy man wearing a suit approaching him. Napoleon messed his underwear from the shock.

The suited man told Napoleon that his name was Death and that his time for collection had come.

Napoleon was not ready to go. "No," he shouted. "It's not fair, you gave me no warning." He scurried into bed to hide under the sheets. Desperately, he reached out to his wife for reassurance.

Her body felt cold, and she was wearing a suit.

Napoleon and Natalie were returning to their luxury country home after a long exhausting day making money in the city as stockbrokers.

Natalie, the least tired, decided to drive. They stayed awake by telling each other popular biblical stories.

The Long Journey Home

Fifty minutes into their journey, Napoleon asked Natalie in a loud yet calm voice why she was driving on the opposite side of the road. Natalie had fallen asleep.

Natalie awoke to find Napoleon dead beside her and the car lodged between two trees. In her daze she heard an ominous voice whisper; "The Lord giveth and the Lord taketh away."

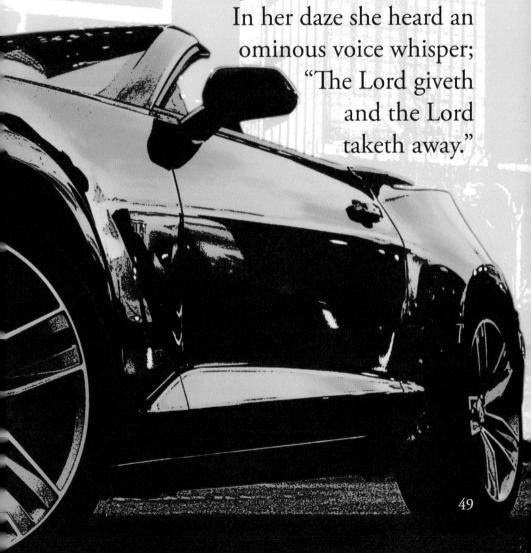

The Price of Inner

Natalie was a mindfulness expert, nurturing her wellbeing practising meditation, reiki and restorative yoga.

Today Natalie's inner peace was broken. A man cycling past kicked her and snatched her handbag.

After the initial shock, Natalie inhaled deeply and on the out-breath chased the robber for 20 kilometres. She caught the exhausted robber, gave him an unforgettable beating, calmly reclaimed her bag, opened her purse which contained $2,000 and gave him five cents and a bottle of water as a lesson of retribution and kindness. Natalie told him, "Never underestimate your victims," giving him another lesson in compassion and understanding.

Peace

Printed
October 2021

Printed in Great Britain
by Amazon